A Bandage for Miss Elaina

Adapted by Haley Hoffman
Based on the screenplay "Miss Elaina's Bandage" written by Saurin Choksi
Poses and layouts by Jason Fruchter

Simon Spotlight
New York   London   Toronto   Sydney   New Delhi

SIMON SPOTLIGHT
An imprint of Simon & Schuster Children's Publishing Division
1230 Avenue of the Americas, New York, New York 10020
This Simon Spotlight edition August 2024
© 2024 The Fred Rogers Company
All rights reserved, including the right of reproduction in whole or in part in any form.
SIMON SPOTLIGHT and colophon are registered trademarks of Simon & Schuster, Inc.
Simon & Schuster: Celebrating 100 Years of Publishing in 2024
For information about special discounts for bulk purchases, please contact Simon & Schuster Special Sales at 1-866-506-1949 or business@simonandschuster.com.
Manufactured in the United States of America 0724 LAK
10 9 8 7 6 5 4 3 2 1
ISBN 978-1-6659-6040-3
ISBN 978-1-6659-6041-0 (ebook)

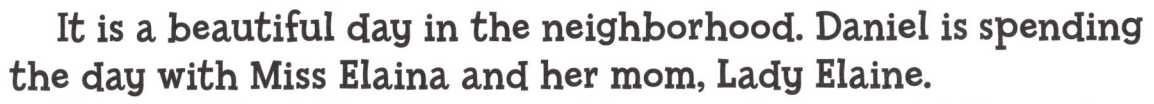

It is a beautiful day in the neighborhood. Daniel is spending the day with Miss Elaina and her mom, Lady Elaine.

"Hi, neighbor! Miss Elaina and I are making music! Tap-a, tap-a, tap-a!" Daniel says.

"I like making music like this. La, la, la!" Miss Elaina says. As Miss Elaina dances, she moves her arms up in the air and accidentally scratches her hand on a tree branch.

"Ouch! Mom, I hurt my hand," Miss Elaina says.
Lady Elaine takes her hand to look at it. "It looks like you have a scratch. We should cover it with a bandage," she says.

Lady Elaine doesn't have a bandage, so she asks Dr. Anna for help. Dr. Anna examines Miss Elaina's scratch.

"I'll go get a bandage from my office," the doctor says.

Dr. Anna returns with some medical supplies. She cleans Miss Elaina's scratch and puts on some cream. This helps Miss Elaina feel better.

"Thank you, Dr. Anna," she says.

"Now let's cover it with a bandage to help it stay clean while it's getting better," Dr. Anna tells her. She pulls a bandage out of her medical bag and puts it on Miss Elaina's hand. "There you go!"

Miss Elaina looks down at the bandage on her hand and frowns.
"What's wrong, Miss Elaina?" Daniel asks. "Is the bandage too big?"

Miss Elaina shakes her head no. "This bandage is too . . . light. It doesn't look like my body. I would like a darker bandage that looks like my skin," she tells Daniel.

Miss Elaina shows her mom her bandage. Lady Elaine grabs Miss Elaina's hand.

"See? That's Mommy's color. Not mine," Miss Elaina says.

"You're right. It doesn't match your beautiful brown skin," Lady Elaine says. She asks Dr. Anna if she has another bandage.

"I'm sorry, Miss Elaina. That's the only bandage color I'm able to find," Dr. Anna tells her.

"Why are there only light-colored bandages?" Miss Elaina asks. "That's a good question," Lady Elaine says. "You should be able to have a bandage that looks like your skin color."

Everyone agrees that they do not think that is fair. They sing,

"When we see something that isn't fair,
we can do something to show we care."

Daniel asks what they can do. Dr. Anna wonders if they can make a bandage that's just right for Miss Elaina.

Miss Elaina grins. "A bandage that looks like . . . me?!"

Lady Elaine has an idea. "The Crayon Factory can make all sorts of colorful things—even bandages! We can go make them right now," she says.

Daniel and Dr. Anna are excited to help!

"We can do it together," Lady Elaine tells everyone.

They hop aboard Trolley and head to the Crayon Factory.

 "We're going to the factory, so we can make new bandages. Won't you ride along with me? Won't you ride along with me?"

Soon they arrive at the Crayon Factory. Lady Elaine shows them a big book of colors. She tells Miss Elaina that they can find the color that matches her skin.

"Thank you, Mommy!" Miss Elaina exclaims.

"Tiger-tastic!" Daniel says.

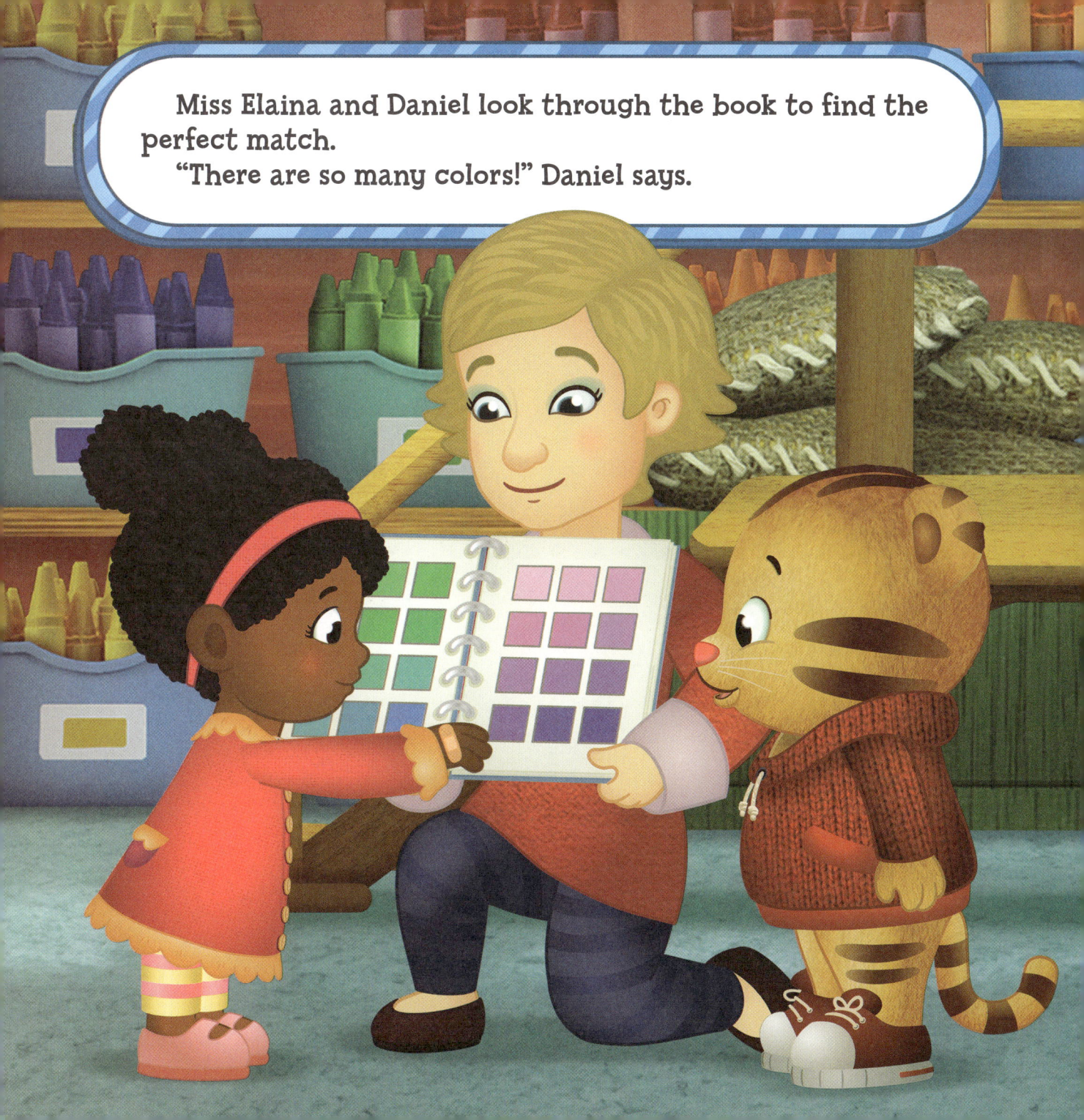

Lady Elaine places the bandage on Miss Elaina's hand. Miss Elaina smiles. "Wow!"

"It looks just like my skin! I love, love, *love* it!" says Miss Elaina. The bandage is just right!

"Thanks to you, now we know how to make more bandages that are just right for me, and our other neighbors, too!" Dr. Anna tells Miss Elaina.